The Song
of
Bones

Dragon Riders of Osnen Book 11

RICHARD FIERCE

Dragonfire Press

Cover design by germancreative.

Cover art by Nimesh Niyomsal

ISBN: 978-1-958354-03-2

CONTENTS

1

I stood atop a tall cliff overlooking an ocean.

As far as my eyes could see there was nothing but clear blue water, the surface reflecting the clouds of the sky overhead. I inched closer to the precipice and looked down. Along the rocky surface of the cliffs were a multitude of shadowy spots. Cave entrances.

I paused. How did I know that? And where was I? This place felt vaguely familiar, but at the same time, it was completely foreign to me.

The Whispering Craggs.

The name drifted in the wind, coming in answer to my silent question. Something had brought me to this place, but …what was it? I looked over my shoulder for Sion, but she wasn't there. A gentle breeze stirred, ruffling my cloak. I turned back toward the ocean and tried to remember why I was here.

The caves.

There it was again. A voice whispering in the wind. Perhaps that's how this place had gotten its name. I turned around and lowered myself over the edge, scaling down the sheer cliff face to one of the cave openings. The air inside was cool and dank and smelled of rotting flesh. I wrinkled my nose in disgust and stepped further into the darkness.

Something shuffled around in the shadows. I laid my hand on the hilt of my sword, my heart quickening. I still couldn't remember why I was here, nor did I know why my feet continued to take me closer to the danger hidden in the gloom. The sound of heavy breathing echoed around me, and before I could draw my blade, the head of a creature came at me, its jaws open in a snarling attack.

I jolted awake.

Sweat covered my entire body, making my clothes stick to my skin. I flung the blanket off and stared at the ceiling, my heart still pounding. It had only been a nightmare, but it was the same dream every night.

"Eldwin?"

I rolled my head to the left and saw Maren's sleepy face scrunched in worry.

"Are you all right?"

"I'm fine," I said. "Bad dream."

"Again?" She scooted closer, laying her hand across my chest.

"You're all sweaty."

"I know."

"Gross."

I patted her hand and rolled out of the bed, stripping my shirt off as I walked over to the window. The panes of glass were foggy, and I rubbed my hand across one of them. The sun was beginning to crest over the horizon.

"Time to get up," I said. "The day is young and we have much to do."

Maren groaned in faux aggravation, but I heard her footsteps as she left the bed and crossed the room to the wardrobe. I pushed the window open slightly, and the cool air that blew in helped dry my skin. I still felt gross, but at least I wasn't wet. A chill ran down my back and I closed the window, turning to look at Maren.

She was dressed and stifled a yawn. A shaft of sunlight slanted through the windowpane, hitting her flowing red hair and making it look like it shimmered with magic.

"Have you ever heard of a place called The Whispering Craggs?"

"Not that I can remember. Why?"

"I think that's the name of the place in my dreams. Every night is the same, but this time, that name came to me."

I walked over and planted a kiss on her cheek before grabbing a tunic from the wardrobe.

"Excuse me, sir. Who said you could kiss me?"

"You did," I replied with a smile.

"When did I say that?"

"When you married me."

"Wait, we're married? I don't remember that."

"You're hilarious."

She wrapped her arms around me and pressed

her lips to mine. Warmth spread throughout my body, pushing the chill away. I slipped the tunic on, and we left the room and headed for the dining hall. The smell of food cooking wafted along the corridor, making my mouth water with anticipation. There was nothing like the meals of the Citadel anywhere else. Just as we reached the entry to the dining hall, Curate Henrik called my name. I glanced back to see him walking toward me.

"Master Anesko wants to see you." He looked at Maren. "Both of you."

"We'll go see him after we eat," I said.

"It sounded urgent. I'd check in with him first in case it's an emergency."

"Very well. Is he in his office?"

"He was a moment ago. I was just there."

"Thank you," Maren said. "We'll go see him. How did yesterday go?"

"It went well," Henrik replied. "The smugglers didn't have any dragons, but we confiscated a large supply of weapons. I'm certain they are connected to the dragon traders somehow."

"Were you able to get any information out of them?"

Henrik shook his head. "No. They wouldn't say anything, even with the threat of Galdrow flaming them. We'll keep them in the dungeon for as long as it takes."

"The noose is closing around them," I said. "I'm

surprised they didn't squeal, though. My contact in Ilok says he thinks there's a small base of operations there. He hasn't been able to confirm the exact location yet, but he has confirmed it's linked to the dragon traders. I think we're close to finally finding something."

"Good work, Eldwin. How many people does your contact say are part of the group in Ilok?"

"He's having trouble getting a firm count, but he's seen at least twenty different faces."

"It would take a decent force to confront them. Master Anesko would want concrete evidence that dragons are being kept there to make a move."

"I know. I'm working on that. As soon as my contact finds the place, he's going to confirm if there are any dragons present. I'm praying for our sake there is. It's difficult to train riders without dragons, and it would be great to bolster our numbers, even by a small amount."

"I couldn't agree more," Henrik said. "I've got to get going. Master Katori and I have something else to investigate."

Maren waved him away and smiled. "The work never ends."

"Indeed."

He turned and left, and I looked longingly at the serving line.

"There's plenty to go around," Maren said. "We can eat after we talk to Master Anesko."

Master Anesko kept the same office after the attack despite the damage the school had suffered. Most of the repairs had been completed, but the other Curates moved to the offices on the opposite end of the school, and I found the silence of the older hall odd even now. Our steps echoed off the walls, and we soon arrived at Anesko's door.

Maren knocked loudly, and I prayed that whatever he had to say wasn't bad.

2

"I'm sure you've both heard the news."

Master Anesko looked over the parchment in his hands, his gaze flicking from me to Maren. We sat across from him.

"You'll need to be more specific," Maren said.

"I would've thought you of all people would have heard, but perhaps you chose not to listen, given the circumstances."

Maren and I exchanged looks, and I saw my confusion echoed in her expression. Master Anesko set his parchment down and rubbed his eyes. He was easily twice as old as me, but his short time serving as master of the Citadel had aged him in ways only a leader could understand.

Overall, his appearance remained much the same as the day I'd first met him. His brown hair was cut short, and he kept his face clean-shaven. His eyes were a vibrant green, and the dark bags under them revealed his lack of sleep. I didn't envy his position. The man seemed to be constantly exhausted, more so than the rest of us.

"The king has requested our aid."

"With what?" Maren asked, frowning.

"A group of his riders has disappeared. It was a routine patrol along the western border. They were supposed to return to the castle two days ago, but they are still missing."

The western border. That was close to Valgaard, Master Hrodin's former domain. The Assembly had rendered judgment on him, and I had no idea where they'd taken him and his dragon. The school had since gone silent, but Master Anesko speculated that Hrodin's son wasn't happy with the way things went.

"Is there any evidence the riders of Valgaard are responsible?" I asked.

"No. That was my first thought as well, but there's nothing implicating them. I'm still investigating the matter just to be certain, but we need to assume at this point it has nothing to do with them."

"My father has many enemies," Maren said. "It's impossible to narrow down who might be behind the disappearance."

"I'm aware of that, which is why I want you two to look into this. You haven't been part of your father's court for a while, but you have the most knowledge of the inner workings. That should give you an edge. The last place they were seen was near Ilok."

My heart skipped a beat. Ilok? Master Anesko met my gaze.

"I've read your reports, and I know what you're thinking. Your primary focus should be to discover what happened to the king's men. *If* you happen across anything else, it should be secondary and only pursued with my approval."

"If I'm right about that place, we're going to need help."

"You can take T'Mere and Feng, but that's all I can spare."

I clenched my jaw to hide my irritation. "Neither one of them has left the Citadel since their bonding. We need experienced riders."

"They are both well trained and will obey your orders as if they came directly from me," Anesko said. "Believe me, I would rather send Curate Henrik and Master Katori, but they are otherwise engaged."

It had been six months since Hrodin's treachery. Those of us who remained had voted to keep the riders from disbanding, but the hunt to find dragons for new students was proving more difficult than I expected. It didn't help that Anesko had us tackling less important tasks like this one, but it wasn't his fault. We were stretched beyond our limits. Rebuilding took time and resources, and we lacked both equally.

I could've argued further, but I chose to keep my mouth shut. Maren and I had promised to obey his rules, and this was one way to prove I could do so, even if I didn't like it.

"As you command," I said.

Anesko smiled at me, seeming pleased I didn't debate him further.

"We'll leave immediately," Maren said.

"Food first," I interjected. "I could smell the sausage cooking on the way here."

"Eat and get any supplies you think you might need," Anesko said. "Don't be ill-prepared for what awaits."

"Breakfast it is, then," Maren said. She rose from her chair.

"I'll meet you in the dining hall. I need to speak with Anesko about something."

Maren's brow rose curiously, but she nodded and left. I waited until I could no longer hear her footsteps before speaking.

"As you know, I've been trying to track down the maker of the dragon bone flutes," I said. "It would help if I could go to the grave—"

"Forget it," Master Anesko interrupted, shaking his head. "The location of the dragon graveyard is forbidden to all but schoolmasters."

I sat back in my chair with a frustrated sigh.

"Someone knows where it is. That's the only place where dragon bones are found. Whoever is making the bone flutes must get them from there."

"I don't think so, Eldwin. The graveyard is protected by powerful wards."

"Have the wards been checked? They could have gotten past the spells when magic was failing."

"I understand your concern with the flutes,"

Anesko said. "But until we have something more than a wild theory to go on, you need to put this matter aside. There are many other things that require your attention."

Anesko was right. There were many things demanding my focus, but for some reason I couldn't explain, I *needed* to find the flute maker and stop them. The flutes not only gave the user more concentrated magic, but they were a desecration of the dead dragons' remains. It angered me, but that anger was deeper than my own bias. I suspected it was coming from the bond, streaming into me from Sion.

"Is there anything else?"

"Yes, actually. Have you ever heard of a place called The Whispering Craggs?" I asked.

Anesko's brows furrowed in thought, but he shook his head. "It doesn't sound familiar. Why?"

"I've been dreaming about this place for two weeks now, and the dream is always the same. It's not a place I've ever been to or heard of. I don't know what it means or why it keeps recurring."

"Maybe it's caused by stress. Is something bothering you?"

"No. At least, not that I'm aware of."

"It could be nothing, but sometimes dreams have a deeper meaning. I'll see if I can find anything about the place. You said it was called The Whispering Craggs?"

I nodded, and Anesko grabbed a quill and scribbled the name down on a spare parchment.

"I'll let you know if I find anything."

"Thank you."

I stood and left his office. My stomach rumbled with hunger, but a sudden thought occurred to me. The library held an extensive number of books on a myriad of topics. Perhaps if the place in my dream was real, I would find something about it there. I paused. Food or knowledge? I turned away from the dining hall and headed for the library.

The door was open for convenience, and I strode in and went straight to the index cabinet. Surrel was busy returning books to their proper locations, and I waved at her when she glanced at me. She smiled and waved back. I scanned the index cabinet for the drawer labeled WH and pulled it out, then flipped through the cards.

There was one record for The Whispering Craggs. My eyes widened. It was an actual place. I wrote the location on a piece of parchment and closed the drawer. That there was a mention of it at all shocked me, but how and why was I dreaming of it remained a mystery. Maybe Sion could provide some clues. I would have to ask her on our way to Ilok.

I found the book I needed and flipped through the pages. It was a long, confusing poem, but it seemed to chronicle a group of people from a distant land with a forgotten name. It read like a history, but none of it was familiar to me. I continued scanning the pages and found the mention of The Whispering Craggs:

The Wild Ones are found at the Whispering Craggs, their numbers too great to count.

"Son of Matthias," Surrel said lowly. "You must have found something interesting."

I looked up from the book. She was the only one who called me that.

"Why do you say that?" I asked.

"The look on your face was one of rapt attention."

I laughed and closed the book, then slid it back into place on the shelf.

"I'm trying to find information on a place I've never been to. This book is the only one in the index that mentions it, but the information is less than helpful. Have you read this one?"

Surrel tilted her head to the side to read the title and shook her head. "I'm afraid not. What is the name of this place?"

"The Whispering Craggs. I've been dreaming about it for some reason. The only mention in this book is that the Wild Ones are found there, whatever that means."

"That's certainly intriguing," she said. "I'm sorry I can't be of more help, but I wish you luck in your quest for knowledge."

"Thanks."

I left the library and went to the dining hall. Maren was sitting at one of the tables, her tray empty. She looked up as I entered and frowned. I hurried through the serving line and took a seat beside her.

"Were you talking to Anesko this whole time? I was just about to come looking for you."

"Sorry," I replied, taking a bite from a soft doughy biscuit. It was smothered in butter, and the creamy rich sweetness buried my tastebuds under a river of euphoria. "I stopped by the library after I was done."

Maren stared at me expectantly. "And? What's going on?"

"Nothing," I said, shrugging.

"You're lying."

I couldn't stop the smile from spreading across my lips. "You know me too well. I want to know why I'm dreaming of the place. Anesko thinks it's from stress, but it's not. The library confirmed it exists."

"Where is it?"

"I don't know. There was only one book that mentioned it, and it didn't say where it was located."

"Do you think it might be Tyrval trying to tell you something?"

I paused in my chewing.

"Gods, I hope not."

3

Sion and I flew side by side with Demris and Maren while T'Mere and Feng flew behind us, following our lead. Feng was from Terran, one of the few members of the school to answer Katori's call to come to Osnen. T'Mere was from the last group of students at the Citadel that had the chance to bond with a dragon. I didn't have anything against them, they were just too inexperienced.

Feng's dragon reminded me of Kage's. It was a Terran dragon: wingless, with scales as black as night. Like Feng, it was a rarity. Many of the Terran dragons had perished when magic failed, but Feng's was one of the lucky ones. T'Mere's dragon was green, smaller and slimmer than others of the same color I'd seen. I assumed it was young. That, or it had stopped growing for some reason.

As we flew toward Ilok, I tried not to think about my dream and the possibility that the Assembly might be trying to pull me into something else, but my curiosity got the better of me.

The dreams haven't let up, I told Sion.

You said it keeps recurring. Everything that happens in the dream is the same each time?

Yes, it's always the same place and everything happens the same way, except for last night. I learned the name of the place. The Whispering Craggs. When I checked the library, I found it's an actual location, but I don't know where it is. There was something else, too.

What?

The book mentioned something called the Wild Ones, but there were no other details. Does that mean anything to you?

No. Do you think it could refer to the creature from your dreams?

Possibly.

I had considered that, but it was only speculation. The book didn't describe what a Wild One was, and the shadows always hid the beast in my dream. Still, it didn't seem to be a coincidence. Maybe Sion was on to something. The mystery remained, though. Why was I having these dreams?

I pushed the troubling thoughts to the back of my mind. We had a task to do, and dwelling on them was only distracting me. We soon reached Ilok and landed outside the city. I dismounted and waited for the others, and we entered the city gates together. Ilok wasn't as big as Tiradale, but it was a decent amount of ground to cover.

"We should split up," I said, looking at T'Mere and Feng. "You two can start with the taverns. That's where people are more likely to let things slip. Maren and I will hit the marketplace. Let's meet back here in an hour."

"Yes, sir," Feng said, bowing his head toward me. The two men wandered off to the right, and Maren looked at me.

"You just don't want to deal with them."

I shrugged. "It's not that. Sending them to the taverns will serve two purposes."

"Which are?"

"Well, for one, we'll see if we can trust them on their own in a tavern. If they come back drunk, we'll know the answer to that."

"Fair enough. And the other?"

"It will give them some experience with the people outside of the Citadel."

"You do realize they had lives before coming to the school, right?" Maren asked.

"Yes, but they won't be treated the same now that they are dragon riders. The people's trust in the Order has been shaken too many times. It's going to be an uphill climb in getting it back."

"Seems like you've put a lot of thought into it. You sure you didn't send them off because you didn't want to babysit them?"

"Maybe that was a small part," I admitted with a grin.

"I knew it."

We reached the market and began questioning people. Most of them ignored us and went about their business. I was used to the reaction at this point. Master Anesko had tried to keep things quiet regarding the failing of magic, but people liked to talk, including riders. And then the battle with Kage and Hrodin happened.

It was obvious people blamed us for their problems, but I took it all in stride. If I had learned anything over the last few months, it was that dwelling on your mistakes didn't help. You could either learn from them and do better, or wallow in self-pity, and I had done more than enough of the latter. We passed a vendor that was selling candied treats, and a customer, a man, looked up as we approached.

"Dragon riders," he said. It sounded like less of a question and more of a statement.

"Indeed," I answered.

"Seems like there's a lot of you coming through here lately."

Maren and I exchanged looks.

"You saw riders come through here?" I asked.

"I did. A whole entourage of them. That was a couple of days ago."

"Are they still here?"

"They didn't stop," he replied. "They flew over the city and kept going."

"Which way?"

The man pointed west.

"Thank you," Maren said. The man nodded and walked away.

"There's nothing out there."

"Except Valgaard," I replied. "But why would your father's riders go there?"

"They wouldn't."

"We should probably check it out, then. Maybe they got lost out there somewhere."

"Or maybe they turned south and just haven't made it back home yet. If they took the long route, it would take them at least four days, and that's if they were flying fast."

I nodded. It seemed likely that was what had happened, but I knew Anesko would want confirmation that we hadn't found anything.

"Let's get the other two and head out."

T'Mere and Feng were waiting for us at the gates, and it surprised me to see they hadn't gotten into trouble. They were sober, too, which told me they could be trusted on their own. That was good.

"We've got a lead, so we're going to check it out. Come on."

We left the city and returned to our dragons, then headed further west. There wasn't much to see past Ilok except wide grassy fields and the occasional animal that sprinted off at the sight of the dragons. Before the battle with Kage and Hrodin, I had an aversion to being pulled into adventures. They usually resulted in something bad happening, and sometimes because Maren and I were at fault.

In the time that had passed since then, I'd begun to enjoy the tasks Master Anesko gave Maren and me. I think the reason I hated it before was because I just wanted a normal life, but long hours of contemplation led me to realize there was no such thing as normal life. There was just life. And I decided I would enjoy every moment of it, no matter what happened, good or ill. And so far, things had been good.

We covered a few miles of ground before Sion noticed something.

Look, she said. *I see a camp.*

I squinted down at the landscape and spotted it, though I couldn't make out the details from our distance.

What are they doing?

Our bond flooded with her concern.

Nothing. The dragons are lying still. I don't see their riders.

They're probably resting, I said. *Take us down.*

Sion descended, and the others followed our lead. We landed outside the camp and a foul odor filled my nostrils. I grimaced and looked at Maren. Judging by her disgusted look, she smelled it, too.

"Gods, what is that?" T'Mere asked. "It smells like—"

"Something died," Maren interrupted.

I dismounted and drew my sword, though I wasn't sure what to expect. It certainly smelled like death. We approached the camp cautiously. There were no signs of movement, and when we got nearer, the horrible truth was revealed.

The dragons were dead. All of them.

I motioned to T'Mere and Feng. "Check the tents."

They both hurriedly obeyed, and I walked over to the closest dragon. Between the stench and the rotting flesh, it was apparent it had been dead for a few days. The sky was clear and the sun beat down on the corpses, which meant the heat had likely quickened the decomposition process. Maren came to stand beside me.

"Look."

She pointed at a gaping wound in the dragon's neck. I knelt to get a closer look, but the flesh was too damaged to determine what may have caused it. I was almost certain about one thing, though. They hadn't died of natural causes. My suspicion was confirmed a moment later when T'Mere stepped out from one of the tents, his face pale.

"The riders are dead. Throats were cut."

Feng exited the other tent and shook his head. "These men are also dead."

"These riders were well-trained soldiers," I said lowly, looking at Maren. "How did someone sneak up on them? And how did they manage to kill ten dragons without raising an alarm?"

"Magic, most likely," she answered. "But whoever did it isn't just powerful. They're depraved."

"There are more questions than answers. They

were in the middle of nowhere. Whoever did this must have been following them. This was planned. Any ideas on who would want to kill your dad's soldiers?"

Maren shook her head. "He has made plenty of enemies over the years, but I can't think of anyone offhand that would have been able to pull this off. I could be wrong, but I don't think an enemy of the crown orchestrated this attack."

I looked back at the dragon corpse and studied it. A scale was missing from its side, and I noticed a long gash that was mostly hidden by dry blood. I held my breath and used my sword to push the folds of flesh apart. I frowned.

"Notice anything odd here?"

Maren drew closer and peered into the wound.

"Some of the bones are missing."

4

We returned to Ilok, my heart heavy. Even though I didn't know those soldiers or their dragons, death was never something I enjoyed seeing. We landed in the same spot we had earlier, and I noticed the city guards atop the walls gave us more than a passing glance.

"We've got eyes," I said, nodding toward the city.

"They're probably wondering why we've come back," Maren replied. "Seeing dragon riders twice within a few days might seem worrisome."

"That's fair. We just need to keep our heads down and not give them a reason to bother us. Master Anesko needs to know what happened, but I think we should remain here to see what he wants us to do. Can you reach him from here?"

Maren shook her head.

"We're too far from the Citadel, but I saw a dovecote we could use."

"What's a dovecote?" Feng asked.

"It's a structure that holds messenger birds. We can send word back to Master Anesko using one of them, but it'll take a few days to get a reply," Maren answered.

I nodded, having already considered our next step.

"We'll take a room at one of the inns and wait for further orders. I don't know what Master Anesko might want us to do, but it's better than going back just to turn around again. Why don't you two go secure our rooms?"

I pulled a few coins from the purse at my belt and handed them to T'Mere. He took them and started walking toward the nearest building.

"Not that one," I said.

He gave me a curious look, but changed direction and headed for a different inn. Feng walked with him, and Maren stared at me expectantly.

"Do you know something about that place that I don't?"

"That's where Rasmus gets most of his information."

"Your contact who's watching for the dragon traders?"

I nodded.

"You should go with them. I need to talk with Rasmus, and I don't know if he'll speak with me if you're there."

"Why? Because I'm a woman?"

"Yes."

"Are you serious?"

I smiled. "Yes, but it's not for the reason you think. He's shy. Had a sheltered life, I guess."

Maren's brows creased, and I knew she thought I was pulling a prank on her. I wasn't, but she didn't need to know the real reason Rasmus wouldn't talk if she was present.

"It won't take me long."

"Fine, but I'm getting something to eat without you. I'm starved."

I fished a few more coins out of my purse and gave them to her. It's not like it was my money. This trip was being funded by the king, with the Citadel being a proxy. He could afford it.

"I'll eat when I'm done here."

I watched Maren leave, then turned to look at the inn. A sign hung over the door, the lettering of its name freshly painted. *The Salty Wolf.* That was the place Rasmus had mentioned in his letters. The name was odd, but it looked well-kept from the outside. I made my way to the door and stepped inside.

The place was busy. Loud voices carried on the air, mingling with the lively tune of a minstrel who played on a small platform in the corner. No one seemed to pay attention to him, but he strummed his song anyway. The interior was just as tidy as the exterior, and the atmosphere was upbeat, jovial even.

There was no fire burning in the hearth, but it was uncomfortably warm. Several scantily clad young women delivered tankards to the waiting patrons, and I glanced around, looking for Rasmus.

He was hard to miss. He sat near the bar, his back to the wall, sipping ale. I strode over to his table and smiled as I took a seat across from him.

"Eldwin! What are you doing here?"

"I'm in the area for unrelated business," I said. "Thought I'd drop in and see if you have any news since your last letter."

Rasmus was larger than me and more muscular. He sported a shaved head, and the skin of his pate was creased so badly it looked like the innards of his skull were showing. His eyebrows were thick and wild, the black strands seeming undecided in which way they should collectively flow, and a handlebar mustache with flared ends curled ridiculously close to his nostrils. Many hoop earrings, gold and silver, lined both of his ears.

To any unsuspecting passerby, Rasmus appeared to be nothing more than an eccentric man. In reality, he was a deadly force to be reckoned with. I'd met him a few weeks ago while investigating a lead on the dragon traders. He had done some work for them and offered to help me in exchange for a favor.

"Actually, I was just about to send you a bird as soon as I finished my drink." He leaned forward and lowered his voice. "I've found the safe house."

Excitement welled within me. Finally, all the hours and effort had paid off.

"It's here, in the city?" I asked.

Rasmus nodded, his earrings swaying with the

movement. His eyes scanned the room behind me, but he continued.

"Aye, it's here all right, but I'll warn you. They've got plenty of men on hand."

I assumed as much. They knew we were closing in on their operations, and it would not be easy to take them down. I'd have to inform Master Anesko so he could send more riders, but it would help if I had detailed information to give him.

"Can you show me where it is?"

"I can, but first, what of our agreement?"

"What you ask for is not easily obtained."

"Neither was what you asked for, yet I still delivered."

Rasmus wasn't cheap, and he wasn't someone I wanted as an enemy. He'd asked for a hefty sum in exchange for his help, and I didn't have it. At least, not in my own pocket.

"Will half get me the location?"

Rasmus glowered at me. "Half covers my work in finding the place. You shouldn't have agreed to the price if you couldn't get me the money."

"Calm down," I said. "I have it. There's extra for your troubles, too."

I untied the purse on my belt and set it on the table between us. The king's gold more than covered his fee. I just hoped no one questioned where it all went. Rasmus slid the purse closer and peered inside. He grinned, and the bag disappeared into the folds of his coat.

"Good man. Give me some time to map out the area. A day or two."

"You aren't going to show me where it is?"

"Not in person. They know my face, and I don't want them to see me snooping around in their business. I'll get you a map with what I know and you can do with it as you will."

"How do I know you aren't going to run off with my money?"

"I may be a scoundrel, but I'm not a thief," Rasmus replied. "Besides, I didn't do this on my own. My counterpart has been inside the place, so he'll have to draw the map. He left town recently, but he's due back any day now."

I supposed it was a good thing I had already paid for our rooms before handing him the rest of the money.

"Fine," I said. "I'll be here for a few days, anyway. I'm staying across the street. As soon as you have the map, let me know."

"Yes, sir," Ramus mocked, bowing his head slightly. He laughed and took another drink of his ale. "You're welcome to hang around. We can be friends outside of business."

"As much as I would enjoy that, I have to get back. I'll be waiting to hear from you."

Rasmus waved a shooing motion with his hands and I left the inn, hoping he wasn't lying to me. He'd been honest up to this point, but money had a way of changing people.

5

It took two days for Rasmus to deliver a rough hand-drawn map.

A knock on the door interrupted my sleepy reverie and I had to climb over Maren to get out of the bed. I opened the door and was greeted by one of the barmaids. She was about a foot shorter than me, with flowing blond hair and bright blue eyes.

"This is for you," she said, holding up a sealed parchment. Even her voice seemed small.

"Thank you."

I took it and closed the door, then broke the seal and unfolded the paper. The map was crudely drawn, but there were enough details that I could decipher it. A large 'X' was marked at the end of the market street to signify the building the dragon traders were using.

"Is it from Master Anesko?" Maren asked.

"No, it's from Rasmus."

After meeting with him, I sent a second message to Anesko asking for permission to investigate the building. I wasn't sure if he was going to respond to my query in the same response to Maren's message, but I had my answer a moment later when there was another knock at the door. It was the same barmaid.

"You must be important," she said, her eyes trailing up and down my body.

"That one is hers," I said, hooking a thumb behind me.

She peered past me and saw Maren, then her demeanor changed and she made an awkward curtsey and left. I turned around and Maren shook her head, a smile on her face. I handed her the letter and sat on the edge of the bed. She opened it and read over the words, then passed it to me.

I apologize for the delay in my reply. I had to consult with the king. He wants you to do an in-depth look at the campsite. No detail is too small. Feng will be helpful with this task, as he has a certain way with magic. As for Eldwin's request, the answer is no. Complete the task at hand.

"What request is he talking about?"

"Rasmus told me where the dragon traders are."

"If you think we should do something, then I'm with you."

I wanted to do something, but I'd given Anesko my word that I would obey his orders from now on. Of course, he didn't have to know if we just got a quick look at the traders' operations.

You're asking for trouble, Sion said, listening to my thoughts.

You're only in trouble if you get caught, I replied. *And I don't intend to be.*

"The first thing we'll do is go back to the campsite," I said. "Any idea what Anesko is talking about regarding Feng?"

"No. I don't really know much about him."

"Me either. I suppose it's time to find out. Meet me in the common room when you're ready."

I pulled my boots on and left, stopping at Feng and T'Mere's room to let them know the plan, then I headed downstairs and ordered us all something to eat. Maren was the first to join me, and we ate in silence, watching and listening to the few patrons who were in the tavern this early. The general attitude toward us was one of concealed displeasure.

"I know why they don't like us," I said lowly, "but do you think they'll ever see us in high regard again?"

"People's memories are short," Maren said between mouthfuls of eggs. "It'll take time, and plenty of effort on our end, but I'm sure they'll come around."

"What if they don't?"

"Then we'll continue to serve them as we always have, but it will be without thanks. I'm all right with that. Doing what's right doesn't require validation."

While that was true, it felt good to know people appreciated what you did for them. I had risked my life several times for the people of Osnen, whether they knew it or not, and something as simple as appreciation went a long way. Perhaps we had lost their trust completely. And if that was true, then perhaps Anesko should have disbanded the riders. Now I understood why he'd considered it. T'Mere and Feng joined us, and I pushed the dark thoughts aside.

"Master Anesko said you have a way with magic that will help us in looking through the camp. What is he talking about?" I asked.

"As you know, sometimes riders gain access to magic they didn't have without the bond. Such was my fate, and I have an unusual talent. I can conjure the past."

"Meaning what, exactly?"

"It means he can show us what happened to my father's riders," Maren said. "We'll be able to see how it all played out."

That was impressive. Maren was a powerful sorcerer, but even she wasn't able to do that.

"We need more people with that ability."

"It comes at a cost," Feng replied. "I'll be weak for a few hours."

"We can carry you back here, if that's what it takes. Are you able to do anything else unusual, like see through walls or anything?"

"I'm afraid not."

I nodded. That was too bad. I didn't want to completely disobey Anesko, but it appeared that was unavoidable. After Feng and T'Mere finished eating, we left the city and returned to our dragons, then went back to the campsite we'd found. The bodies remained the same, but the stench seemed to have worsened. I prayed for a breeze, but the gods weren't listening.

Feng buried his nose into the crook of his right elbow and stood in the middle of the camp. He stretched his left hand out and closed his eyes. For a long moment, nothing happened. I grew impatient and wondered if he could see anything before I noticed movement. It was faint at first, but white ethereal outlines materialized. It was the king's riders. They were setting up camp. A few of them erected the tents, while the others talked among themselves. Their mouths moved, but there was no sound.

The scene blurred, and then the riders were gone. Their dragons were lying where the corpses rested now, the ghostly figures appearing as if their souls were wavering free of them. Light shined within the tents, and then they went dark. Everything blurred again, and then a host of armored figures stealthily entered the camp. There were a dozen of them, and the group split into two. One went toward the tents while the other converged on the dragons.

The sleeping behemoths didn't move at all. I found it hard to believe they didn't hear the approaching steps, no matter how quietly they moved. They probably had help to conceal themselves. Likely magic, as Maren had assumed.

My stomach churned as I watched the first dragon die. One of the figures plunged a sword into its chest. Now I knew for certain magic was involved. No ordinary blade could hurt a dragon. Their hide was too strong, their scales even more so. They murdered the other dragons right after the first, none of them uttering a single sound as they died. I looked at the tents. The figures stepped out of them, their deeds obvious. They rummaged through the camp and then faded from sight.

Something didn't make any sense. Bones were missing from the dragons, yet their killers hadn't touched the bodies other than to kill them. The spectral images blurred yet again. The seconds passed, turning to minutes. I held my tongue for fear of breaking Feng's concentration. The images cleared, and I watched intently, refusing to exhale.

Another figure appeared. This one wasn't wearing armor. Was he unrelated to others? He strode up to one of the dragons and pulled a dagger from his waist, then slashed the blade across the creature's side. More magical weapons. He pushed his hand into the wound, and a moment later, removed a bone. He did the same thing to the other dragons, placing his prizes in a bag slung across his shoulder. The apparition left, and the entire scene faded.

"What did we just watch?" T'Mere asked. "Who were those people?"

I looked at Maren. She shook her head slightly. If she didn't recognize them, then we had nothing to go on. And there was the other figure, the man who took the dragon bones. Had he happened upon them, or was he part of the whole thing?

"I'm left with more questions than answers," I said. "We'll let Master Anesko know what transpired. Did anyone recognize that last person?"

"Maybe he's from Ilok," T'Mere suggested. "We could search the city for him."

It was a good idea, but it wasn't feasible. I shook my head.

"That would be like searching for a grain of sugar in an hourglass. It could take weeks, assuming he's even in the city, and I don't think he is."

"Why not?"

"That's not something to concern yourself with," I said. "It's something we're investigating separately."

Weird dreams, dragon traders, the mysterious bone flute maker, and now this. Things were quickly getting out of hand. I looked at Sion, suddenly worried for her safety. If there was one thing we didn't need, it was dragon slayers.

6

After we returned to Ilok once again, Maren sent a letter to Master Anesko. We had to help Feng walk because of the exhaustion his spell casting had caused, but it wasn't long before he could support himself, and we gathered at the end of the market street.

The building on the map was directly ahead of us. I didn't see any guards, but I was certain the place was being carefully watched.

"We're going to gather some information about the dragon trader operations. They've got the advantage here, so we will not try to take them down. I just want to confirm this is one of their locations and see if they are holding any dragons captive."

Rasmus guaranteed me it did indeed belong to them, but I wanted to confirm it for myself before letting Anesko know.

"What are we looking for?" T'Mere asked.

"Signs of dragons mainly, but take note of anything else. How many people you see, if they are armed. Things like that." I looked at Feng. "Are you feeling all right? If not, you can wait at the inn."

"I can manage," he said.

"If you say so. You and T'Mere go around the back. Maren and I will take the front. If you get caught, just feign ignorance. Under no circumstances should you reveal you are riders."

"Understood."

"Good. You two go ahead."

I waited until T'Mere and Feng disappeared around the corner of the building before nodding at Maren. We casually walked along the street, turning to the right. As we rounded the front of the place, I saw a lone figure standing beside the main doors. It was Rasmus. I paused, my thoughts all jumbled as I tried to figure out what he was doing here. He grinned, and there was something about his expression that told me he'd betrayed me. I glanced around and noticed several men approaching from various directions.

"We've got a problem," I said, looking at Maren.

"Let me guess. Your contact isn't as trustworthy as you thought?"

"Sorry."

I drew my sword and took a defensive stance, hoping that T'Mere and Feng weren't in the same predicament. I couldn't believe Rasmus had tricked me. We'd spent months working together. How could I have been so blind?

"Put down the sword, Eldwin." Rasmus walked toward me. He was still smiling, but there was no humor in his eyes.

"Why? Why now?"

"Don't get me wrong, my boy. I didn't intend to sell you out, but my presence here didn't go unnoticed. They grabbed me after I delivered the map. It was death or rat you out. I chose to save my own skin."

The knowledge that he hadn't willingly betrayed me offered some solace, but it didn't matter. It was still his fault. If he'd been more careful—

"Drop it and they might let you live," Rasmus said, lowering his voice as he got closer. The other men had now surrounded us, and they were all carrying swords.

"You know I can't do that," I replied. "You should leave while you can. Maren here is a sorcerer."

Rasmus looked at her. Maren lifted her right hand and wiggled her fingers at him. He shook his head.

"You're insane, but I get it. I didn't go down without a fight, either." He turned his head to the side, and I saw a fresh gash and bruising along his neck. "Best of luck to you, Eldwin. I'm sure we'll see each other again if you survive."

With that, he left, retreating quickly down the road we'd come down. I turned to face the others, stepping in front of Maren to block her with my body.

"Are we taking prisoners?" she asked.

I thought about the constant nightmares Sion experienced because of the torture she'd received at the hands of similar men, and the answer was obvious.

"No."

Before I could register what was happening, a bright flash of light filled the air, blinding me. A roar like thunder echoed off the surrounding buildings, and I reached back and grabbed onto Maren with my free hand. The ground trembled beneath my feet, and the men around us cried out. The light faded, and after my vision cleared, I saw that all of them were on the ground, unmoving.

Every time I blinked, I saw the bright light again. I looked at Maren. Her expression was severe.

"Did you stun them?"

"Into eternity," she replied. "We need to get T'Mere and Feng and get out of here."

I didn't disagree. We sprinted around to the back of the building, but the two men were nowhere to be found. There was a raucous inside the building. I tried to pull the door open, but it didn't budge.

"Move," Maren said.

I stepped aside and she lifted her hand, whispering a few words under her breath. The air visibly rippled, and an invisible force blew the door inward, splitting it in half. Wooden splinters showered the floor, and I rushed into the building. T'Mere was on the ground and Feng was kneeling beside him. Three bodies lay on the ground nearby, and a host of armed men were quickly approaching from the front of the building.

"Help me carry him," I told Feng.

He looked up at me and shook his head. A pool of blood was slowly growing around T'Mere. His eyes stared off into oblivion, and I knew the terrible truth. I swallowed hard. Maren cast a spell, the magic flickering through the air as it sailed past us and struck the approaching men. It dropped them all.

"We need to go," Maren said. "Before the city guards arrive."

"What about T'Mere?" Feng asked. "We can't leave him here."

I knelt and pressed my fingers to T'Mere's neck. There was no pulse.

"He's gone. We'll come back for him."

"You think they are going to leave his body here?"

"I don't know," I said. "Come on."

Feng rose, his expression hard to read. Maren led the way out of the building, and we turned the corner to find more trouble. A dozen guards, dressed similar to the ones inside, came at us, weapons drawn. I pushed ahead of Maren and met the first one, our blades clanging loudly as they connected.

From my periphery, I saw Feng engage another guard. I pushed my opponent back and swung my sword left to right, knocking his blade free of his grasp. It skittered across the cobblestone street and his eyes widened in fear. I hesitated for just a moment before cutting him down. The next two fell just as easily, and I realized these men weren't trained soldiers, they were simple thugs.

Feng was a blur of motion, and his fighting style was very similar to Master Katori's. She must have trained him personally. Half of the men had fallen, and those who remained quickly turned and ran. Feng started to chase after them, but I held him back.

"Let them flee," I said. "Justice will come to them, one way or another."

He relented, and we left in the opposite direction, hurrying along the street and returning to the inn. Feng went to his room, but Maren and I took a seat at one of the tables. Now that the adrenaline rush was gone, guilt overwhelmed me. T'Mere would still be alive if I hadn't disobeyed Anesko. I could feel Maren staring at me, and I met her gaze.

"You couldn't leave it alone, could you?"

I frowned. "You said you backed my decision."

"Yeah, *I* did. You didn't give T'Mere the option. You asked Feng, but only because he was too weak to do much."

My throat tightened, which worked in my favor because it kept me from trying to say anything. I sighed through my nose and rested my head in my hands until the feeling subsided.

"It's my fault," I said. "I take ownership of that, and I will face Master Anesko's judgment, whatever it may be."

"That's great, Eldwin, but that doesn't bring T'Mere back, does it?"

I had seen Maren angry before, but never at me. I wasn't sure how to respond, so I said nothing. She wasn't wrong in her anger. I had failed, not only T'Mere, but myself as well. What kind of leader got someone under his command killed? Maren rose from her chair and headed for our rented room, leaving me alone with my remorse.

7

The next morning, Maren still wasn't speaking to me. We had slept in the same bed, but she'd kept to her side and ignored me. It was the first time we'd argued about something so serious, and I didn't know how long it would take her to forgive me. To be fair, I didn't know how long it would take to forgive myself.

I pushed the foggy remnants of my constant odd dream aside and left the room to eat a quick meal, then exited the inn and wandered along the city streets. It was midmorning, and the people of Ilok were already roaming about, buying and selling goods, food, and other things. I passed The Salty Wolf and considered going inside, but I knew Rasmus wouldn't be there. He was probably long gone by now. He'd run off with a large sum of money, and I was back at the beginning of my quest to find the dragon traders. I had found one of their buildings, true, but I hadn't seen any dragons inside nor any signs that there had ever been any.

Do not blame yourself for his betrayal, Sion said.

I should have been more vigilant, I replied. *T'Mere is dead because of me. If I had obeyed Anesko's orders, he'd still be here.*

When have you ever done as you're told?

All the time until I met Maren.

Sion probed my memories. *Do you truly believe that?*

The image of me as a child sneaking a treat from a tray my mother had prepared flashed in my mind's eye, and I knew Sion was intentionally showing it to me.

Fine, most *of the time I follow instructions.*

Sion's mirth flooded the bond. *You are not good at lying.*

I was lost in our conversation and not paying any heed to where I was going until I noticed the ambient sounds of the city had lessened. A glance at my surroundings revealed I was at the end of the market street. I turned my gaze to the building we'd been at the day before and stood there for a long moment.

I know what you are considering. You shouldn't go in there alone.

Since when do I do what I'm supposed to? I asked, smiling and thinking myself clever.

There were no guards or signs that anything had changed at the building, but it had seemed empty yesterday and that assumption had proved disastrous. I rested my hand on the hilt of my sword and walked around the back of the building. The doors Maren had blown apart had not been replaced, and I saw T'Mere's body lying in the same spot he'd fallen the day previous.

I swallowed hard and stepped inside. It was quiet. Had the remaining traders left, or had we killed them all, leaving their hired hands to abandon the place? I walked past T'Mere's corpse, stepping lightly as if I could somehow disturb his eternal rest. The interior of the building was spacious, but it was mostly empty. I frowned. There was nothing here to indicate the place belonged to the traders, and yet, they had been guarding it.

But why?

As I walked toward the front of the building, the boards under my feet creaked. I paused and looked down. A rectangular line was faintly visible along the floor. It was a trapdoor. I knelt and ran my fingers along the wood until I found the hidden latch. It opened smoothly and I lifted the door up. Below, torchlight flickered, illuminating the darkness. Against my better judgment, I climbed down the ladder and into the tunnel. It had been carved into the dirt and ran the length of the building, possibly further.

I drew my sword and stepped softly. Torches lined the wall on the right side, spaced every six feet or so.

I've found something, I told Sion. *I'll warn you if I run into trouble. That way you can tell Demris where I am and Maren can rescue me.*

Shouldn't it be the other way around?

You'd think so.

Sion chortled through the bond and I couldn't help but smile despite the possible danger. I tightened my grip on the hilt of my sword and continued further along the tunnel. There was a chamber on the left and I could hear voices speaking within.

"I'm getting tired of waiting," someone said. "Our shift should have ended hours ago. Where are the replacements?"

"I haven't heard anything up there in a while. Maybe they forgot about us."

"It's not like these blasted things can't take care of themselves."

The other one grumbled his agreement. I pressed myself against the wall and risked a glance through the doorless archway. There were three men. The two talking were sitting at a table and the third was slumped on the floor, an empty bottle lying near him.

"I think they're more worried about them escaping than being cared for. As long as they pay us extra, I don't care how long I'm down here. It's better than being at home with the wife. All she does is complain."

Were they talking about dragons? I looked down the hall to see if there was another chamber doorway, and the tip of my sword scraped against the ground.

"Did you hear that? I think someone's coming to relieve us."

I cursed under my breath and struggled to sheath my blade. Footsteps signaled the approach of someone. I finally slid my blade back into the scabbard and stepped into the archway, startling the man.

"Morning," I greeted. "Sorry for the delay. We had some issues that needed to be dealt with."

The man eyed me, his gaze fixating on my maimed arm. "Who are you?" he asked. "I've never seen you before."

I didn't see any reason to lie about my name. "I'm new here. The name's Eldwin. They sent me down here to relieve you."

The man looked past me into the hall. "Who's with you? There's always supposed to be at least two of us on duty."

"It's just me. Everyone else has been pulled away."

It quickly became apparent this wasn't going to end well. Aside from the wary and distrustful look he was giving me, I couldn't let them leave. They'd find T'Mere's body and know something was amiss.

"What's with him?" I asked, nodding toward the man lying prone on the ground.

"He's drunk, as usual. Who do you report to, Eldwin?"

"Uh …"

The other guard, the one sitting at the table, stood up quickly and drew his sword. "He's not one of us!"

I lifted my hands placatingly. "Calm down. I

don't remember his name."

"What did he look like, then? Describe him."

If these two were as badly trained as the ones I fought yesterday, I had no doubt I could take them both. I squinted and looked to the right as if trying to remember. They both stared at me expectantly. Without second-guessing myself, I lifted my right leg and kicked the nearest man in the stomach. He staggered backward into the table, knocking it over and falling to the ground. The other man managed to jump out of the way and rushed me.

I drew my sword and stepped forward, parrying his attack. I forced his blade out wide and drew mine back, slicing a long line across his chest. He wasn't wearing armor, and blood soaked through his tunic.

"Surrender," I said.

He dropped his sword and grabbed at his chest, grunting in pain. The one I'd kicked into the table rose to his feet and picked up one of the table legs that had broken off. He came at me, swinging the thing like a madman. I brought my sword up to block him and sheared the table leg in half, then rolled my wrist to bring the blade back around. I pressed the tip of my sword to his neck.

"Do you yield?"

"Who are you?"

"Don't worry about that. Answer my questions and I'll let you live."

The two men exchanged looks and the one clutching his chest nodded. The one at my mercy sighed. "What do you want to know?"

"What are you doing down here?"

"Guarding the cargo until it departs."

"And what cargo would that be?"

He clenched his jaw. "Why do you want to know?"

"I'm asking the questions," I reminded, prodding him with the sword.

"Dragons," he hissed. A droplet of blood ran down his collarbone.

"How many?"

"Ten."

"Are they in good health?"

"They wouldn't be of value otherwise, would they?"

I smirked, but there was no humor. At least, not toward him. After months of work, I'd finally found what I'd been searching for. The network of the dragon traders was vast, but this was a start.

"Where else are dragons kept?" I asked.

"What do you mean?"

"Places like this. Where are the others?"

"I don't know. The people in charge keep a lot of secrets."

I flicked my gaze from one man to the other, trying to decide what to do with them. They were criminals and didn't deserve to enjoy their freedom, but I couldn't just kill them.

Tell Demris I need Maren's help, I told Sion.

8

While I waited for Maren, I forced the two men to sit beside their unconscious fellow. They glared at me. I had the upper hand and they knew it. I swept my gaze around the room. A triangular shelf with dry goods was in one corner, and bedrolls were laid out on the opposite side.

"Where are the dragons kept?" I asked.

"There's a bigger room at the end of the tunnel," the injured one said.

"How do you get them in and out of here?"

They both stared mutely at me. I took a step toward them.

"They come here as eggs and remain here until they're sold or until they get too big."

"What happens if they get too big?"

"They get sent somewhere with more room."

"How do you get them out? Where's the exit?"

"You can't take them," the other one said. "The way out is protected by magic. That's why the dragons don't leave on their own."

I wasn't worried about that. Maren was more than capable of handling whatever spells they had in place. What concerned me was the state the dragons were in and how they would respond to being freed. The last thing we needed was for them to ravage the city, taking their wrath out on the innocent people of Ilok. Sion was the best suited to speak with them, considering she'd once been in the same predicament.

There was noise in the tunnel, but I wasn't sure if it was Maren. I strode over to the men and pointed my sword at one of them and waited. My heart thudded double time and relief washed over me when Maren and Feng entered the archway. Maren looked from me to the guards.

"There *are* dragons here," I said. "Ten of them."

Maren's expression changed from veiled anger to surprise. "Where are they?"

"At the end of the tunnel. I haven't seen them yet, but I think Sion should be the one to talk to them first. It might go over better with them since we don't know what they've been through."

"What about them?" she asked.

"We can hand them over to the local constabulary or bring them back to the Citadel and let Master Anesko deal with them. The latter seems better to me. It'll give us the chance to interrogate them further and keep them from warning the others."

"You said you'd let us live if we told you what we knew!"

I jabbed the one that spoke with the tip of my sword. "You can live in a dungeon."

He looked away from me, silently fuming.

"We need to bind them," I said. "Do you see any rope?"

Feng walked over to the shelf in the corner and rummaged around. Maren joined me and gave me a look that told me she was still upset. I accepted the wordless scolding without complaint.

"This should work," Feng said as he returned with some braided cord. He cut a few pieces and used the rope to bind each man's wrists behind their backs, including the unconscious one.

"Watch them," I said, then sheathed my sword and grabbed onto Maren's hand. I led her out of the room and down the hall. It was roughly a hundred feet before we came to a wooden door.

"What were you thinking coming back here?" Maren demanded.

"I didn't plan on it. I was just walking around the city talking with Sion, and the next thing I knew, I was here."

"You could have turned around."

"If I had, then I wouldn't have found the trapdoor."

"Eldwin." Maren's features softened. "Master Anesko is going to be furious with you. You gave him your word. We both did."

"What is he going to do? Kick me out of the school?" I scoffed. "We're struggling to continue our duties as it is. He needs us all too much."

Maren shook her head. "I know that tracking

down these traders means a lot to you, but you can't risk everything you have in the pursuit. It will only impede your search even more."

"Do you remember when we were trying to find Demris?" I asked. "You were so passionate about stopping him from hurting people, and you were confident that he wasn't doing it on purpose. You refused to give up."

"I know."

"That is how I feel. I found Sion with a group of people like this. They treated her horribly. And it's not just about helping them. It's about keeping the riders from disbanding. We voted not to, but you and I both know there's no future for the Order if there are no dragons."

"I'm not saying I don't agree with you," Maren said. "I just want you to do it the right way. If we don't have Master Anesko's support, we'll never succeed."

She was right, but my pride kept me from admitting it. I didn't *need* Anesko's support. I'd done many things on my own, without the help of the school, like finding Sion. If I had to do this on my own, then so be it.

I admire your strength, but I agree with Maren, Sion said. *You will not get far without the Citadel. You and I alone are not enough to find the traders and stop them.*

I closed my eyes and sighed, the invisible weight of so many things on my shoulders.

"I'm sorry." The words were as much for Maren as they were for Sion. I tried the handle. It was unlocked, and I pushed the door open and stepped inside. Floating near the ceiling was a giant globe of orange light. It lit up the chamber, which was more like a cavern, and bathed everything in a warm glow.

Several dragons were lying on the ground, basking in the light. I counted nine in total. Had the guards lied to me, or miscounted? It didn't really matter. We'd found them, and soon they would be well taken care of at the Citadel.

"There's an exit somewhere in here, but it's warded with magic." I looked over my shoulder at Maren. "Before you unweave the spells, we need to figure out where the exit leads. Sion can wait on the other end and make sure none of them gets past her."

"That's a good plan."

"Those are the only kind I have."

Maren rolled her eyes and pushed past me into the chamber. If the dragons were aware of our presence, which I assumed they were, they acted as if they didn't notice. I followed Maren as she walked along the wall of the room. The dirt glowed with a faint light, which I knew was the result of magic. When had the traders built this place? And had the loss of magic affected them when the souls had been siphoning it? I could only guess.

"Look there," Maren said, pointing.

There was an opening in the wall, but it was hidden by shadows. The glow of the orange globe couldn't seem to penetrate the darkness. I suspected the gloom was part of the wards that prevented the dragons from escaping. We walked closer. At the other end of the opening, I could see daylight.

"Can you tell if the spells will keep me from going through?"

Maren closed her eyes and lifted her hand, palm facing toward the opening. After a moment, she lowered her arm and looked at me.

"The wards are only intended for the dragons."

I looked back at the creatures and spotted one I hadn't seen before. It sat in the shadows, watching us intently. I turned back to Maren.

"I'm going to get Sion. Once she's in place, we can figure out the rest."

The opening appeared normal, but I knew the dangers that magic presented. I hoped Maren was right about the spells. I took a few hesitant steps and nothing happened. Satisfied, I hurried through the tunnel and stepped out under the sun. I was outside the walls of Ilok. Clever. The traders had a way in and out that allowed them to avoid the suspicion of the city guard.

I need you over here, I told Sion.

I'm coming.

A moment later, I saw her red bulk fly over the city. She turned toward me and descended, landing nearby.

There are dragons in there, I told her. *I need you to convince them to come to the Citadel with us.*

Sion's tail swayed behind her, and she tilted her head to the side. I could feel her curiosity flowing through the bond.

I will do what I can, she said.

I returned to the chamber and nodded at Maren. She mirrored the gesture, then began her work. The dragon who'd taken an interest in us was still watching. The other dragons stirred, lifting their heads to look at us. I swallowed hard, not sure what to expect.

"It's done," Maren said.

The dragon in the shadows sprang forward like a pouncing cat. I threw myself against Maren, pushing her out of the way. We tumbled to the ground, and a thunderous roar echoed through the chamber.

9

The roar came from Sion.

I rolled over and sat up. The dragon from the shadows backed away from the tunnel. Now that it was in the open, I saw its scales were black. No wonder I had missed it earlier. Its ebon color had blended in with its surroundings.

Sion's head emerged from the opening, a deep, rumbling growl coming from her chest. The black dragon continued to back away until it ran into another of the creatures. The others were on their feet, warily watching Sion's approach. There was no way to hear the conversation, but I knew Sion was speaking with them.

"Did I hurt you?" I asked lowly, looking at Maren.

"I'm fine," she replied.

I nodded and slowly got to my feet, then offered her my hand. She took it and I pulled her up. We remained where we were, waiting for Sion to confirm everything was under control. She was twice the size of the other dragons, and they all seemed to be afraid of her. Of the ten dragons, most of them were blue. There was the one black dragon, and two were red like Sion.

"I agree with you that we should take the guards to Anesko. I just don't know that interrogating them will be a priority for him."

"If interrogating them leads to finding more dragons, I think it will sway Anesko," I said. "He knows we need dragons more than anyone."

All is well, Sion's voice entered my mind. *They are skittish because of their treatment, but they have decided to trust me.*

Good work, I told her. *Are they strong enough to fly?*

They will need to take many breaks, but yes, they can fly.

"We're all set," I said, looking at Maren. "They will come with us."

She smiled at me. "That's ten new riders. Perhaps Anesko won't be too angry."

We returned to the first room where Feng was watching the others. The drunken man was awake now, and he looked haggard and confused.

"We're taking them to the Citadel. Master Anesko will decide their fates."

"On your feet," Feng demanded, forcing each of them up. I took charge of the wounded one, and Maren took the drunkard.

"We need to keep them separated so they don't try anything. Can your dragon hold both of you?"

"Yes," Feng answered.

"Good."

I walked over to the broken table and gathered several parchments that were strewn about. A glance revealed they were reports of some kind, so I took them. We led our prisoners into the chamber with the dragons, then out through the tunnel. We waited for Demris and Feng's dragon, whose name I didn't know, to join us. T'Mere's dragon refused to answer anyone, but Sion eventually coaxed her into joining us.

The dragon was hurting and wanted nothing to do with anyone. I didn't blame her. When my bond with Sion had been taken on the Island of Lost Souls, it had been devastating. I'd almost given up on life.

"Did anyone leave anything at the inn?" I asked.

"No," Feng replied.

Maren shook her head.

"Then I think it's best we get going. Take the lead," I told Maren. "I'll catch up with you."

"What are you doing?"

"I can't leave T'Mere's body to rot in there. Sion and I will lay him to rest."

Maren stared at me for a long moment, then nodded. "I'll try not to fly too fast. I wouldn't want you to cry about being so far behind." She smiled playfully, and I rolled my eyes at her.

"One of these days, Sion is going to leave Demris in the dust and then we'll see who's gloating."

"You can dream," she replied.

She climbed onto Demris's back, and I helped

boost her prisoner up. He sat in front of her so she could keep an eye on him, and then I helped Feng next. Once they were situated, they took to the air. The other dragons followed after them, and soon it was just me, Sion, and my injured charge.

I'll be back shortly. If this one moves, fry him.

Don't tempt me, Sion said.

I went back into the cave and returned to the empty building. T'Mere's corpse was still there, and I briefly wondered why the city guard hadn't come to investigate the day previous. Perhaps they hadn't heard the raucous, or maybe they didn't care to get involved in rider business. I pushed the thought away.

T'Mere was about my size, so I assumed it would be easy to carry him. I couldn't have been more wrong. He was dead weight, no pun intended, and I struggled to get him over my shoulder. It took several tries, and I had to use every ounce of strength I had, but I finally managed to lift him. My plan had been to take him out through the cave, but that wasn't going to work. I'd end up falling down the ladder or dropping him, and I didn't like the idea of either.

I have to take him through the city, I said. *Hopefully, the guards mind their own business.*

Do you want me to meet you at the main gates?

I stepped out of the busted doorway and into the city. There had to be another way out, one less crowded, but I couldn't exactly go looking for one while carrying a dead body. Not to mention he was heavy.

Change of plans, I said. *Let's burn the building. It'll remove the stain of the traders and send T'Mere to his rest.*

Is that the wisest idea?

It's the easiest.

What if the fire spreads?

That seems unlikely. This place isn't near anything else, which I suspect is why the traders chose to use it.

I took T'Mere back inside and laid him down, then placed his arms across his chest. I stared at his face for a long moment, the guilt washing over me again.

"Gods," I whispered. "I'm sorry, T'Mere."

I rose and left, heading back down underground and through the tunnels. All I could think about was how he'd still be alive if it wasn't for my poor decision making. I deserved whatever Anesko's punishment was. Upon returning to Sion, I mounted up, keeping my prisoner in front of me as Maren had. Sion launched into the air and flew over the city, pausing over the trader building long enough to issue a long gout of flame that set the structure ablaze. Satisfied it would burn to the ground, Sion sped over the landscape to catch up with Maren and the others.

It didn't take long before their enormous shapes

came into view. We zipped ahead of them and flew beside Demris. I nodded at Maren, and she smiled in return. I was glad to see her anger had faded. The feeling of uneasiness I felt in my spirit when she was upset unsettled me. It was something I didn't want to experience ever again.

We had to stop several times to allow the young dragons a reprieve. According to Sion, they were regularly underfed, on purpose, to keep their energy levels low. It made them easier to control. All the extra stops made the trip back to the Citadel take much longer than I expected, but I didn't want to push the dragons too hard. They'd been through enough, and it wasn't like there was a pressing need to return quickly. I was just impatient.

All humans are impatient. It's because of your short lifespans.

Don't remind me, I said. *What will you do when I die?*

I don't know. It isn't something I've considered before.

I'm afraid to die.

The thought had always hovered in the back of my mind, but I'd never admitted it to myself or anyone else before.

Why?

There are so many things in this life I want to do and experience. That, and ... I don't know. It's just a scary thought. Given all that I've seen, the afterlife is so uncertain. What end lies for me if I don't end up on the Island of Lost Souls? Where do I go? What happens?

Life holds many uncertainties, death many more so. You will never know until your time comes.

I didn't enjoy thinking about such things, and I told her so.

Very well. What is that man doing? I feel him moving around.

I looked down and saw his wrists were still tightly bound. He didn't seem to be moving to me. I peered over his shoulder and saw his head was slumped down.

I think he's sleeping.

Sion's doubt filled my mind.

No, he's doing something.

I leaned forward to look again, and the man slammed his head into my face, sending me reeling back. Pain exploded in my nose and made my eyes water, but my vision was clear enough to see the man jerk to the side as he threw himself off Sion's back. I sat forward and reached for him, but I wasn't quick enough.

He went spinning through the sky.

10

Hold on, Sion said. She dived sharply, and my stomach churned. It was a feeling that I could never get accustomed to, no matter how many times I experienced it. I spotted the man, a speck compared to the mass of the approaching ground.

We dropped fast, but the distance between us was too great. Sion roared and pulled her wings tightly against her body. It was too late. She was forced to pull up, and I averted my eyes as the man struck the earth.

He would rather die than face Master Anesko, I said.

Or perhaps he feared his masters would think he betrayed them.

Why would he fear their retribution? He would have lived the rest of his days in the dungeon.

That doesn't mean they wouldn't have been able to reach him there. They are more resourceful than you know.

Sion returned to Demris's side, and I shook my head in response to Maren's questioning gaze. Neither of the other two men tried to follow their friend's example, and we reached the grounds of the Citadel without further incident. The guards and stable hands alike gawked in surprise at the arrival of the new dragons, and pride swelled within me.

We did good, I told Sion.

We shall see what Master Anesko says.

Indeed.

I dismounted and paused. There were riders positioned around the courtyard I didn't recognize, and then I noticed the king's emblem on their armor. I looked at Maren. Her expression was unmistakable. She was not happy.

"Do you think your father is here?" I asked.

"Unfortunately, yes."

She climbed down Demris's shoulder and strode angrily into the school. I watched her go, uncertain how things would go between Maren and her father. She hadn't spoken to him since she'd invoked the Right of Secession, giving up her royalty to be with me. I hurried over to the nearest guard.

"Get these dragons into the stable and provide them with food and water," I said.

"Yes, Curate Eldwin." He bowed and rushed off to obey.

Let them know they are being taken care of.

I already did, Sion said. *They are still wary, but they trust me. I will make sure they have what they need.*

Thank you.

I entered the school and made my way toward Master Anesko's office. I assumed he would host the king there. Curate Henrik intercepted me in the hall, his face grim.

"The king is here," he said.

"I figured as much. What does he want?"

Henrik shrugged. "I'm guessing it has to do with his missing riders. Did you find anything?"

"Anesko didn't tell you?"

"No. Katori and I returned a few hours ago and I haven't had time to turn in our report yet."

"The riders were murdered, but we're not sure who did it. We also rescued some dragons from the traders."

Henrik's brow rose in surprise. "Your contact was right, then?"

"It's a long story, but yes. I'll fill you in after I talk with Anesko."

"Very well. Good luck with the king."

I smiled and continued down the hall. My memory of Maren's father was not a good one. He'd threatened me, calling me nothing more than the dirt beneath his feet. I was not looking forward to seeing him again. I turned down the hall that led to Anesko's office and saw Maren.

"Wait for me," I called out.

She looked back and halted her steps.

"Are you all right?"

"I haven't seen him in so long," Maren said. "And despite that, my anger burns even still. I can't promise I will be civil."

I shrugged. "Don't be. You don't owe him anything."

"No, but he is the king. Now that I'm basically a commoner, he could execute me if he wanted to."

"He wouldn't do that. And even if he tried, I wouldn't let him. He'd have to kill me first."

"I love you, Eldwin, but let's be realistic. He's the king. He could raze the school if he wanted and there's nothing anyone could do about it."

She was right, but that didn't mean we would go down without a fight. As egotistical as he was, I didn't believe Erling was daft enough to do something as crazy as execute his own flesh and blood.

"Take a breath. Go in composed. If he sees you're already flustered, you know he'll take advantage of that."

Maren nodded. She leaned in close and kissed me gently on the lips, then grabbed my hand and we entered Master Anesko's office together. Erling was lounging in a chair in front of Anesko's desk, surrounded by a ring of armed guards. Anesko stood behind the desk, his hands clasped behind his back. He looked at us as we entered.

"Your Majesty, we have company. Eldwin and Maren Baines."

Erling stood up and turned to face us. He looked exactly the same as I remembered. An extravagant crown that sparkled with gemstones adorned his bald head. A gray goatee thinned past his chin and stretched up the sides of his face, ending evenly near the tops of his ears. Beginning in the middle of his forehead and running the length of the left side of his face was a blotchy, red-purplish bruise.

"Your Majesty," I said, sweeping into a low bow. Maren also bowed, but she didn't greet him.

Erling glanced from me to Maren, then returned to his seat. Anesko motioned for us to join them, and we did so.

"I was just briefing His Majesty on your latest report from Ilok. I didn't know you had returned already."

"We just arrived," I replied. "I've got a lot to tell you."

"Is there any new information regarding the royal riders?"

"No, sir. Our attention was diverted elsewhere after our second visit to their camp."

Anesko's stare told me he knew I had gone against his command, but he didn't say anything.

"I trust the money my steward sent was plenty more than you needed," Erling said. "I'll take the rest back now."

"We lost it," I said.

"What?" Maren whispered.

"*I* lost it," I clarified. "Forgive my clumsiness, Your Majesty."

"These are the sort of people you put in charge around here?" he asked Anesko. He tsked. "Perhaps I should install a new leader."

Anesko's expression hardened. He was too disciplined to offer a retort, but I knew he wanted to leap over the desk and strangle the man.

"It was a simple mistake," he said. "Eldwin will repay the money."

"Yes, of course."

I wasn't sure if Anesko really intended for me to or if he was just playing the king's game. Either way, the king wasn't likely to get his money back any time soon. It would take me years to earn the sum needed to repay him. Unless I tracked Rasmus down and he miraculously didn't spend any of it.

"You're indebted to the kingdom," Erling said, casting a disapproving glance at me. "Not a suitable position to be in."

"If that is all, we have a report to share with Master Anesko," Maren said. I could tell by her tone that she was on the verge of losing control of her anger.

"Anything you need to share with your master, you can say in front of me."

I looked at Anesko for guidance, and he offered a slight nod. If he knew what I had to say, he would not have given me permission. I cleared my throat.

"After we returned from investigating the camp," I paused, knowing Anesko was going to be furious. "We checked the building the dragon traders were using. They attacked us, and we were forced to defend ourselves."

Anesko's jaw clenched. "Continue."

"Maren and I were at the front of the building, and Feng and T'Mere went around the back. After Maren dealt with our attackers, we rejoined Feng and T'Mere and that's when …"

My throat constricted and I coughed several times, trying to finish speaking.

"That's when we saw T'Mere had been killed," Maren said.

Anesko's eyes widened. "What?"

"T'Mere is dead," she repeated. "At the hands of the traders."

Erling was smiling. I clenched my hands into fists, overcome with rage. How could he find the death of someone so amusing? An enemy, sure, but not a rider. Not one of his own subjects.

"I specifically said that you were to leave it alone," Anesko said, looking at me. "You gave me your word that you would obey my orders, and you have failed yet again to do so."

"I'm sorry. I saw an opportunity to get more information, but I didn't intend to do anything. My contact betrayed me. We had no choice but to fight."

"It appears Curate Eldwin has disobeyed a direct order," Erling said. "What is his punishment?"

The king was enjoying this. We all knew it. I waited for Anesko to deny the man his satisfaction.

"Maren, you are dismissed."

I looked at her. She scrunched her face, clearly confused, then met my gaze. She wanted me to give her a sign that I needed her to stay, but I didn't give her one. I could handle Anesko's punishment on my own. It was my decision, and therefore my burden.

"Yes, Master," she said. She took a step and looked at me again, searching my face. I kept my expression stoic, and she nodded and left the office.

"I am at my wits' end," Anesko said. "We have enough problems already, and you present me with more. I have been more than patient, Eldwin. I have turned aside countless punishments for your previous behavior, but I cannot do so any longer. You have no respect for authority, and I will not tolerate it any longer."

His acting was phenomenal. Erling still had a stupid grin on his face, which told me he was eating up the performance. What was he going to say next? What sort of 'punishment' would I receive?

"I have no other option but to suspend you from the school."

11

"What?"

My heart skipped a beat and fell into my stomach. Did he just say that? No, I must have misheard him.

"You are suspended from the school, effective immediately. I'll give you until morning to settle your affairs, and then you must leave."

"You surprise me, Anesko," Erling said. "You *do* have a backbone."

I ignored his remark and stared pleadingly at Anesko, but his angry expression did not change. Where was I supposed to go? The school was my home.

"What about Sion?" I asked.

"She must go with you. Maren is required to remain here."

Erling rose from his chair. "I will take my leave now," he said. "I expect to hear from you immediately if you find anything else regarding the murder of my riders."

"Yes, Your Majesty. I will inform you the moment I have news to report."

"Good." He looked at me, his lip curling in a sneer, and he strode out of the office, his guards falling in tow behind him. After he was gone, I stepped closer to Anesko's desk.

"That was an act, wasn't it?"

Anesko's expression softened, but not much. "No, Eldwin, it was not. You have forced my hand in this matter. I hope you will take this time to learn the importance of obedience. Your punishment is not unjust. T'Mere lost his life because of your actions."

"I know," I mumbled. "I take full responsibility. The guilt I feel is more punishing than your suspension."

"As it should be. It is important to note that this is temporary. You will come back after a short time away. We are too shorthanded for me to ban you forever. Make no mistake, however. I am disappointed in you. I expected you to keep your word."

Relief washed over me and I managed to breathe a little easier. "Thank the gods," I said. "You scared me."

"You don't seem to understand the gravity of what you've done. Your concern lies with being here at the school more than the death of your fellow rider. If I wanted to be cruel, I would send you personally to inform T'Mere's family and let you deal with the consequences. And yet," he sighed and sat in his chair. "I will not do that. Please, Eldwin. You must do as I say if you want to be here."

"It won't happen again," I said.

"You say that every time."

"I know, and I'm sorry for disobeying you. There is something deep inside me that fuels the desire to find the traders. It's probably Sion's desire imprinting on me."

"Be that as it may, you are responsible for your dragon as much as for yourself. If you cannot block her desires from the bond by now, I don't know what to tell you. You've had plenty of training."

"I will speak to her about it. I've neglected to do that for fear that she will be upset with me, but that is something I will have to live with."

Anesko nodded tiredly. "Now tell me about the dragons. How many did you find?"

"Ten," I replied. "They are in the stable. Sion convinced them to come with us, but they aren't likely to warm up to anyone soon. Their captors did not care for them well."

"I'm not surprised. Those who had them only care about keeping them alive for the promise of money."

"There's something else, but I didn't want to say anything while the king was here."

"What is it?"

"Feng's magic revealed someone else visited the rider camp after they were murdered. Whoever it was cut the dragons open to retrieve their bones. I think it was the one responsible for the bone flutes."

"Perhaps they are working together. How else

would this person know where the dragons were?"

"I've considered that as well, but I don't think they are. It was several hours later when he made an appearance, so your question remains: how did he know the dragons were there? I haven't figured that out."

"We will unravel the mystery as more clues come to us. Until then, I want you to forget about the bone flutes. Our primary concern is finding those responsible for the murder of the king's riders. Once that crime is solved, then we will turn our attention to the traders. While your method was flawed, you have proven that it is worthwhile to track them down."

He was proud of me, whether he said the words or not. I nodded.

"You are not to engage in any official rider business while you are suspended. Reflect on your decisions and get some rest. When I call upon you to return, I expect to see a new Eldwin before me."

"Yes, sir. How long am I suspended for?"

"I haven't decided yet. You'll receive word when I want you to return."

What was I supposed to do now? Rest? I didn't know what the word meant anymore.

"You're dismissed. Handle everything you need to and make sure you let Maren know what's happening. I don't need her running off after you. Her duties here cannot be neglected."

I bowed and left the office. If I couldn't engage in any riderly duties, then perhaps I could do my own investigation into the bone flutes. Anesko had suspended me, but he'd also said that wasn't his concern. In other words, the matter wasn't official business. I didn't know if he intended to phrase it that way, but I was going to assume he had.

There was just one problem.

I still didn't know the location of the dragon graveyard. There had to be some clues there, but Anesko refused to divulge anything to me about the place. I had an idea. It was stupid, but technically, I was no longer bound to the rules of the school. The hall intersected, and I took the left corridor and stopped short when I saw Maren.

"What happened in there?" she asked. "My father was grinning as if he'd just left a brothel."

"Anesko suspended me."

Maren gasped. "He can't do that."

"He can, and he did. It's temporary, though, so that's good. I have to leave in the morning."

"I'm coming with you."

"You know I would love that, but you can't. Anesko needs you here."

"He needs you here, too."

"Yes, but I left him with no other option. T'Mere is dead because of *me,* not anyone else. I will accept his judgment, and you should as well."

While that was true, I also didn't want her to

know what I was planning. I felt guilty about hiding my intentions from her, but it was for the best. The less I shared with anyone, including her, the better.

"Fine," she said. "But I won't pretend to be happy about it."

I chuckled. "I wouldn't expect anything different. I've got a few things to do in preparation for leaving, so I'll see you tonight."

Maren pulled me close and planted a kiss on my lips. I returned the gesture, and then we broke apart and she walked away. I was going to miss her, but hopefully, my suspension wouldn't last long. As Anesko said, he was too shorthanded to lose any of us.

I went to the stable and retrieved the papers I'd taken from the safehouse. They were stuffed in Sion's saddle, and I took them to the library and spread them out. Most of them were useless, but I found one that held something interesting. It spoke of someone called the Carver and how to reach him, as well as what type of bones he needed.

Perhaps Anesko had been correct about the connection between the traders and the bone flute maker. I assumed it was a relationship of mutual benefit, though I didn't know what the Carver was providing in exchange for the bones. Flutes perhaps, but it could be anything. I kept the one parchment and trashed the others, then got a bag together with some clothes and provisions.

The evening hours passed uneventfully, and once I was certain Maren was asleep, I slipped out of bed and quietly left the room. I navigated the hallways with soft steps. The torches had been doused, leaving the corridors dark, but I had memorized my way around the school long ago. I could feel Sion's curious mind trying to probe my thoughts, but I kept a wall up against her scrutiny. Surprisingly, she didn't question me.

I stopped outside a door and touched the handle. It was unlocked, just as I had hoped. Had Anesko forgotten to lock it, or was he not worried about anyone rifling through his things? It didn't matter. I pushed the door open and peeked my head inside. The room was dark like the halls. I stepped into the office and closed the door behind me.

It was time to find the location of the dragon graveyard.

12

After an hour of searching Anesko's office, I was forced to give up. I had considered that he wouldn't leave that information in writing anywhere, but how would he have learned of the location considering the master before him, Master Pevus, had been poisoned?

I exited the office and stood in the hallway, trying to decide my next step. The easiest thing to do would be to adhere to Anesko's command of forgetting about the graveyard. If I did that, all of my work to find the mysterious person behind the bone flutes would be for nothing. No, I couldn't give up on the task yet.

Anesko had said that only schoolmasters knew the location. Hrodin was imprisoned by the Assembly, and Anesko refused to share the information. That only left Katori. Would she tell me? Our friendship had grown close during the fight against Kage, but after we returned to the Citadel, we'd both been too busy to talk much.

It was late, but I was unlikely to catch her in the morning. I hurried along the hall and made my way to her chamber. It felt weird to be scurrying around in the middle of the night like some sort of criminal. I knocked on her door and prayed she was awake. A moment later, the door creaked open.

I had always found Katori's exotic appearance

beautiful, but my feelings toward her differed from what I felt toward Maren. With Katori, the attraction I felt was more admiration than anything. She kept her long black hair tied back with a white ribbon. She was shorter than Maren, barely reaching five feet in height. Despite her size, she was a formidable warrior, and not just because she was a sorcerer. Her brown eyes peered out at me and then she opened the door fully.

"Eldwin," she greeted quietly. "What are you doing here?"

"I'm sorry for the late hour, but I need your help."

"With what?"

I lowered my voice. "I need to know where the dragon graveyard is."

Katori stuck her head out of the doorway and glanced left and right, then stepped back and motioned for me to enter. I walked into her room and closed the door. The space was larger than mine and Maren's, but it was sparsely furnished. She spent more time away from the Citadel than I did, but I was certain our way of living was odd to her. In Terran, even the buildings were works of art. Here in Osnen, the architecture was very plain.

"Why do you want to know about the graveyard?"

I explained everything that had happened over the last few days to her. If she had been asleep before I knocked, I could not tell. She was alert, and her clothing wasn't disheveled at all. When I was done, she stared at me in silence for a long while.

"Anesko told me the knowledge of the graveyards is only given to masters. He doesn't believe the wards were affected when magic was disrupted. I believe otherwise."

"He has probably checked the wards and confirmed they are still in place," Katori said.

"Possibly, but I am certain the flute maker is getting some of the bones from the graveyard."

"Why do you think so?"

"I found a parchment at the trader warehouse that said he needs specific bones from a dragon for the flute. Since most dragons serve the Order, it seems unlikely he would find what he needs anywhere else."

"You provide convincing evidence, but I am sorry, Eldwin. I cannot tell you where the graveyards are."

"Graveyards? There's more than one?"

"There are three that I know of," Katori replied. "My oath to secrecy prevents me from revealing anything else."

There were three schools, so three graveyards made sense. Well, there used to be three schools. The Terran school was no more, and Valgaard had gone silent since Hrodin's imprisonment, so that really only left the Citadel.

"Is there anything else I can help you with?"

I shook my head. "No. My apologies again for bothering you so late."

"It is no trouble. I will see you when you return from your suspension."

"Anesko told you?"

"He did. You would do well to learn to obey his instruction."

Of course, he told her. He probably told the Curates as well. I supposed there was no reason to keep it a secret, but it embarrassed me that everyone knew.

"I hope you have been well," I said, changing the subject.

"I have. And you?"

"As well as can be expected."

"Very good. You should go now."

"Of course. Thank you for listening to me."

I left, more defeated now than before. If I couldn't go to the graveyard, then I would have to find the Carver himself. The parchment detailed how to get ahold of him, so I wasn't at a complete loss. I just needed to change plans. I returned to my room. Maren was still asleep, and I slipped into the bed and laid beside her, resting my arm over her.

It seemed as though the moment I fell asleep, Maren moved and woke me up. She kissed me on the cheek and got out of bed. Morning light filtered through the window, and I knew it was time for me to leave. I rose and dressed in my armor, then strapped my sword at my waist. Maren embraced me in silence, and we held each other for a long moment.

"This isn't goodbye," I said. "I'll be back. Soon, hopefully."

"I know," she whispered.

We parted, and I headed for the door, pausing long enough to look back at her one more time before leaving. I retrieved the bag I'd prepared the previous day and went to the stable. Sion was waiting for me, saddled and ready to go.

Will they be all right without you? I asked her, nodding toward the other dragons.

They should be. I told them I would return in a few days and to trust that the humans here would keep them safe.

Good. They are the hope for our future. Anesko will take good care of them.

Where are we going? she asked.

To find the Carver.

Sion probed my memories as she stepped out of her cave. I strapped my bag to the saddle and climbed up her shoulder, seating myself.

He is the one who makes the flutes?

I think so. The parchment I read seems to imply that.

Where do we find him?

We first have to find one of his messengers. The

traders have a presence in Tiradale, so we will go there.

What do the traders have to do with the Carver? Sion asked.

They are working together somehow.

Sion growled, and the sound vibrated through the saddle against my legs, tickling me. Stepping out of the stable, Sion stretched her wings wide and took to the air. We rose higher and higher, turning west and leaving the school behind.

I had been to Tiradale a few times over the last six months, though it was mostly day trips to handle minor disputes. My investigation into the traders there had yielded little results. I'd confirmed they worked out of the city, but I hadn't been able to find anyone willing to spy on them for me as I had in Ilok. For some, money wasn't worth the risk.

Several hours later, we landed outside the city and I dismounted. I rubbed the scales along Sion's neck and she hummed pleasantly.

Who is the messenger?

I don't know, I said. *And I don't need to. They have a system of communication that I plan to use to my advantage.*

Clever.

I am, aren't I?

Sion was not amused by my humor. I shrugged. *I'll let you know if I need your help.*

I'm going to hunt down some food, she replied.

I'll keep close enough to hear you.

I headed for the gates. The guards on duty glanced at me briefly. This was the only place where the people didn't show their outright distrust or hatred of us. I supposed it was because Maren and I had saved Baron Giffor's daughter, as well as many of the commoner children. They had no reason to believe the ill rumors because they had seen our deeds for themselves.

The city streets were busy, and I followed the flow of foot traffic until I found the place I was looking for. A windowless building that towered above the surrounding structures. At the top was a dovecote. I broke away from the crowd and entered the building. An older man, gray-haired with spectacles, looked up as I entered.

"Good day," he greeted. "Sending or receiving?"

"Sending," I replied.

"Where to?"

"Here locally."

"I see. It'll be one gold piece. What's the message?"

I'd brought what little money I had stashed away at the Citadel with me and fished a single coin out and set it on his desk.

"Ivory awaits the gentle hand," I said, repeating what I'd read from the parchment.

The man scribbled it down in a smooth script

and rolled the paper up, tying it with a red ribbon.

"Who is it for?"

"The Helper."

"From?"

"Leave it blank. The receiver will know."

"Very good, sir. Anything else?"

"That's all."

The man set the letter in a clay vase atop the desk. I stepped back outside and walked across the street, taking up a position where I could see the entrance to the dovecote.

"Now we wait," I muttered to myself.

13

Based on what I'd read, the Helper was a messenger that informed the Carver a bone had been found for him. The Helper would then leave a return message with where the bone should be left. What I didn't know was whether the Carver retrieved the bone or if it was the Helper. Either way, I hoped to have one of them to interrogate by the end of the night.

I watched the dovecote for a while, counting the number of visitors and noting their clothing. After an hour, I went back inside the building to check if my message had been taken yet. It was gone. The old man behind the desk handed me a rolled parchment and continued with his work. I pulled it open and read the words.

The instructions were to leave the bone at an abandoned building near the wall that surrounded the castle. I thanked the old man and left. Now I just needed a bone. I headed for the market district and found a large bone that had been discarded by a butcher. It was a bit small, but I planned on hiding it in a sack. I took it and found a vendor selling produce that had a cloth sack I could use. I offered a coin for her trouble, but she refused my money and let me have it for free.

I walked along the street that led to the castle and spotted what I assumed was the abandoned building mentioned in the letter. The smell of freshly baked bread reached my nostrils, and I looked to my left to see the baker's shop. I'd spoken to the man who ran it when Maren and I had been investigating the children that had disappeared. A glance through the window revealed he was in there working now. I continued walking and stopped in front of the building at the end of the row.

A sign posted in the window said the building was available to rent. I looked around to make sure no one was watching, then forced the door open and went inside. The wood floor shined under the slanted rays of sunlight that filtered in through the windows, casting a glare on the ceiling. I wasn't sure where to leave the decoy bone, so I set the sack atop a long cabinet against the wall.

I didn't think anyone had followed me, but I decided not to leave anything to chance. I left out the same way, then walked up the street and circled to the back alley and returned to the building. The rear door was locked, but I was able to open a window and climb inside. So far, everything was going according to plan. Once again, I watched and waited.

The time slipped by, and I grew bored. I wondered if anyone would show up, thinking maybe I had somehow made a mistake. A sudden thud startled me, and I placed my hand on the hilt of my sword. The sound had come from the back of the building. I remained hidden, and a moment later, a man strode into the front room and grabbed the sack. He slung it over his shoulder and went back the way he'd come. I quietly drew my sword and followed after him. As soon as he reached the window, I prodded the tip of my blade into his back.

"Who are you?" I asked.

"Who's asking?"

My instinct was to announce I was a dragon rider, but I caught myself.

"I'm asking the questions. Are you the Carver?"

The man burst into a fit of laughter. He dropped the bag and lifted his hands, slowly turning to face me. The man was young, probably around my age. His hair was short, the color of coal, and his brown eyes meet my gaze.

"Am I the Carver, he asks? Me? Ha!"

Was he talking to himself? Perhaps he was insane. I prodded him with my sword again.

"Easy there. If you kill me, it won't get you anywhere."

"I'm not going to kill you," I said. "Not unless you force me to. Are you the Carver or not?"

"I hate to disappoint you, but I am not."

"You're a Helper?"

"Very astute." He grinned at me. His teeth, the ones that were left, were yellow.

"Tell me where the Carver is."

"Why would I do that?"

"Because you don't want to die."

"Ha! What do you know? Nothing! Maybe I do want to die, eh?"

"I can arrange that," I said, growing frustrated.

"Whether I want to live or die doesn't matter, really. I don't know where the Carver is."

"Then how do you get the bones to him?"

"You think I'm a fool, don't you? I may not have all my wits anymore, but that doesn't mean I'll spill my secrets for you."

I looked down at my sword and back at him. He mirrored my movement, then stepped closer, pressing my blade harder against his flesh.

"I do not fear death," he said, his expression becoming serious. "I welcome it."

How do you reason with a madman? I asked Sion.

I would flame him. Or eat him.

I'm not a dragon. And I don't think that would help. Death doesn't faze him.

You'll think of something.

"Why do you seek the Carver? Do you desire a flute?"

"No. I want to stop him from making them."

The man grunted. "You can't."

"Why not?"

"He is clever. You cannot set a trap that he will fall into."

"We'll see about that. How do you get the bones to him?"

"If I tell you, it won't matter. You will never catch him. That bone," he nodded toward the sack, "it's a fake, yes? I thought so. It's too light to belong to a dragon. It won't fool him. He can smell the real ones."

"He can smell them?"

The man inched his left hand over to his face and tapped his nose. "He uses magic to sniff them out."

"Who? Dragons?"

"Indeed."

If the Carver was a sorcerer, it was going to make my task more difficult, but with Sion's help, I was confident we could still take him captive.

"I don't enjoy repeating myself. How do you get the bones to him?"

"I leave them for him to find."

"Where?"

"In the fields where the song can be heard."

"Stop speaking in riddles! Where do you leave the bones?"

"You don't seem to know much about the one you seek. That may turn out bad for you, but that is not my concern. There is a field to the south where the grass grows tall and no man lives. Do you know of it?"

I didn't, but Sion and I could find it easily from the sky. I nodded.

"That is where the song can be heard, but only when the wind blows. Leave a bone there, a *real* dragon bone, and the Carver will come for it."

"That's it?"

"Were you hoping for more?"

"I don't want any surprises," I said.

He grinned again. "Ha! You are in for quite a surprise if you haven't already been there. Are you going to kill me now?"

"I told you I wasn't going to, and I will keep my word." I pulled my sword away from him. "You are free to go."

The man stared at me oddly, then offered an exaggerated bow. "It was a pleasure," he said. "Though I fear your path will end badly."

He whirled around and climbed out of the window, sprinting down the alley. I heaved a sigh and sheathed my blade. That was exhausting. I looked at the sack on the ground. If what he said was true, then my decoy would not work.

The Carver uses magic to find dragon bones, I told Sion. *He can sense if they are real or not. How do we draw him in without a real bone?*

Sion was silent, and I wondered if she was too far away to hear me. A moment later, she replied by filling my mind with an image.

I have an idea.

14

We flew south, scouring the landscape until we found a field that didn't have any settlements nearby. Sion wheeled over the area, but I saw nothing out of the ordinary. Why would the Carver come all the way out here?

Do you see anything?

No, but I sense old magic, Sion said. *Powerful magic. I think it's an illusion spell, but I can't pierce the veil of what it's hiding.*

Take us down. That madman must have been telling the truth.

Sion descended and landed gently on the ground, the wind from her wings rustling the grass. Soft music drifted in the air and I looked around.

Do you hear that?

Yes.

There was nothing for as far as I could see except the swaying field. I dismounted and slid down Sion's shoulder. The grass settled, and the music stopped. I found that curious and grabbed a handful of the strands and shook them.

Nothing.

I tried it again, harder this time. Still nothing. The grass wasn't the source of the music, then.

Where's the illusion?

Right in front of us, Sion replied.

The field is an illusion?

It would seem so. The source of the magic is strongest here.

I strode forward. It was almost imperceptible, but I saw the air ripple slightly. If I didn't know any better, I would think my eyes were playing tricks on me. A few more steps and the scenery changed. The tall grass was still there, but the skeletal remains of dragons lay strewn about. I blinked, hardly believing what I saw. I drew back, and the skeletons disappeared.

You need to see this, I said.

Sion snaked her head forward into the illusion, which created an odd sight. Midway from her neck upward, there was nothing. I stepped forward again, and the bones reappeared.

It's a graveyard for those of my kind who have fallen.

I couldn't believe my luck. I'd found it, or rather, happened upon it. No wonder the Helpers brought the bones here. That meant I was right. The Carver was accessing the graveyard.

The wards must have failed when—

The words died on my lips as I stepped closer. A powerful shock tore through my body, sending me flying backward. I hit the ground with a thud, my vision swimming. My ears were ringing, too. Sion's head appeared above me.

Are you all right?

That hurt.

My muscles spasmed of their own accord. The pain slowly receded, and I sat up. The wards were definitely still up. Then the mystery remained. Why did the Carver come all the way out here to collect the bones? I eased myself back onto my feet and waited for the numbness in my toes to subside.

The illusion hides anything within its boundaries. That will work in our favor, I said. *I'll remain within it during your ruse. Hopefully, it won't take long for the Carver to make an appearance.*

The sight of easy prey may draw him quickly.

That's true. I'm ready when you are.

Sion raked a claw along her underbelly. The wounds weren't too deep, just enough to draw blood. I stood within the illusion and watched as Sion lay on the ground. The Helper said the Carver could smell dragon bones. If that were true, then I hoped he could also smell their blood. The minutes slipped by. Gray clouds gathered overhead.

Looks like rain, I said.

Stay focused, Sion replied. *We don't know what to expect.*

I'm watching, but there isn't much to see.

As if in reply, the ground in front of Sion swelled upward. It rose a few feet and split open to reveal a wiry, thin man with gray hair. I'd been expecting someone sinister-looking, but this person looked … well, normal. He wore a brown tunic and forest green trousers, reminding me of a woodsman. His hair was short and unkempt, as if he'd just awoken and rolled out of bed. Upon seeing Sion, he issued a soft gasp and scrambled backward.

The desecrater, Sion hissed.

What is he doing?

He's afraid.

The man stood still for a long while before slowly creeping closer. "Struggling to stay alive," he muttered to himself. "Your suffering will be over soon," he told Sion.

The old man unsheathed a dagger from his belt and held it above Sion's side. A jewel on the pommel glowed with a sickly green light. He remained in the same position, the movement of his eyes the only sign that he wasn't frozen. It seemed as though he was waiting for something.

A gust of wind blew across the field, and I heard the song again. It was louder than before, and I glanced over my shoulder. The sound was coming from one of the skulls.

It's the bones, I realized. *The song is coming from the bones.*

The bond filled with surprise, both mine and Sion's. The Carver made his move, swinging the dagger downward. Sion sprang up onto her feet and slapped the small man to the ground, pinning him with her claw. I drew my sword and stepped out from the illusion, pressing the tip of the blade to his neck.

"You've been difficult to find," I said. "Neat little trick you did there with the ground."

His eyes were wide, and they remained locked on Sion.

"What's wrong? Never seen one alive before?"

He shook his head slightly. The irony was not lost on me, though I couldn't blame him for being afraid. Dragons were massive, powerful creatures, and they instilled fear in almost everyone.

"This is my bonded, Sion. She wants to know why you've been defiling the bones of her fallen brethren."

"For m-magic," he stuttered.

I stabbed my sword into the ground and knelt beside him. His eyes turned to me and I could see he was more than mildly afraid. He was terrified.

"Explain."

"When magic was d-dying, I experimented to f-find a solution. It was an accident. Dragons are m-magical creatures, and even long after they are d-dead, their bones hum with power. The others found out what I d-discovered and demanded I make more f-flutes."

"Others? What others?"

"The ones who deal in t-trading dragons."

"Why are you still making them if magic has

been restored?"

"The flutes s-strengthen spells, allowing sorcerers to do th-things they couldn't without it."

"Is that how you smell dragon bones?"

"Yes."

I nodded. He seemed harmless, but whether he realized it or not, he was an enemy of dragons and riders alike. I could feel Sion's disgust and hatred for him flowing into the bond.

"How did you get past the wards?" I asked.

"I've n-never entered the graveyard."

"Then where do you get your bones from?"

"They've all come f-from dead dragons in captivity."

"The traders?"

"Y-yes. Mostly."

Anesko had been right on both accounts. I was a fool for not trusting his judgment. Yet despite that, I had tracked the Carver down and had him at my mercy now. At least one good thing had come out of my suspension.

"How many dragons do they have? And where are all the safehouses?"

"They have many," he replied. "But their f-fortresses are no longer safe. S-someone has been breaking in and k-killing the dragons."

I assumed he was referring to Ilok and I shook

my head.

"Sion and I destroyed the safehouse in Ilok. The dragons aren't dead. We took them to the Citadel."

"I don't k-know anything about Ilok. The f-fortresses in Rimshur and Brine were overrun. Every d-dragon was killed."

"By who?"

"I don't k-know who they are," he said. "All I know is they are d-dragon s-slayers. The remaining fortresses have b-been reinforced with more guards. They don't l-like their assets being t-taken away."

I thought about the image Feng's magic had revealed: the armored group who'd massacred the king's riders. That had to be who the Carver was talking about. I stood up and looked at Sion.

I have everything I need from him.

"You are going to die now," I said without looking at the Carver. "May the gods have mercy on you, for Sion will not."

"No, p-please," he stammered.

Sion pressed her claw down, crushing him and forcing his body into the ground. She dug her claws across the earth, burying him with dirt and loose grass. It was a better end than he deserved. I sheathed my blade and climbed into the saddle.

It seemed the riders had a dangerous new enemy to contend with.

THE END OF BOOK 11

ABOUT THE AUTHOR

Richard Fierce is a fantasy and space opera author. He's been writing since childhood, but began publishing in 2007. Since then, he's written multiple novels and short stories.

In 2000, Richard won Poet of the Year for his poem *The Darkness*. He's also one of the creative brains behind the Allatoona Book Festival, a literary event in Acworth, Georgia.

A recovering retail worker, he now works in the tech industry when he's not busy writing.

He's married and has three step-daughters (pray for him), three dogs (huskies!), three cats, two ferrets and a fish. He basically has a zoo.

His love affair with fantasy was born in high school when a friend's mother gave him a copy of *Dragons of Spring Dawning* by Margaret Weis and Tracy Hickman.